"Hey, T. J., look out!" Zack shouted.

T. J. looked up just as a motorcycle swerved to avoid hitting the soccer ball that had bounced out into the street.

"Get that ball out of the street!" the cyclist roared as he sped by T. J.

With a dash and a fast dribble, T. J. rescued the ball and returned to the group of boys on the sidewalk.

"Whew!" T. J.'s best friend, Zack, breathed a sigh of relief. "That was a close call!"

THE FASTEST
CAR IN THE COUNTY

NANCY SIMPSON LEVENE

Chariot Books™
David C. Cook Publishing Co.

Chariot Books™ is an imprint of David C. Cook Publishing Co.
David C. Cook Publishing Co., Elgin, Illinois 60120
David C. Cook Publishing Co., Weston, Ontario
Nova Distribution Ltd., Torquay, England

THE FASTEST CAR IN THE COUNTY
© 1992 by Nancy Simpson Levene for text and Robert Papp for
illustrations

Designed by Elizabeth Thompson
Illustrated by Robert Papp
First Printing, 1992
Printed in the United States of America
96 95 94   5 4

Library of Congress Cataloging-in-Publication Data
Levene, Nancy S.
        The fastest car in the county/Nancy Simpson Levene.
        p. cm.
Summary: T.J. enters his model car in the Pinewood Derby and learns
the value of not taking revenge when others do us harm.
ISBN 1-55513-395-9
[1. Model car racing—Fiction. 2. Revenge—Fiction. 3. Christian
life—Fiction.] I. Title.
PZ7.L5724Fas 1992
[Fic]—dc20   91-33539
                                                    CIP
                                                    AC

To my Lord Jesus Christ Who has given His blessing
to yet another series of books
and to Ed Marquette
who generated the theme of this book
and whose interest and advice enabled it to be written.

Never pay back evil for evil. Do things in such a way
that everyone can see you are honest clear through.

Romans 12:17
The Living Bible

ACKNOWLEDGMENTS

I want to thank Brooks Marquette for sharing his
champion race car design with T.J. Thank you, Patti and
Lara Kupka, for your help and support. A special thanks
to my daughter, Cara, for contributing substantially to
this new series. May God bless all of you!

CONTENTS

1

THE RACE CAR

"Hey, T. J., look out!" Zack shouted.

T. J. looked up just as a motorcycle swerved to avoid hitting the soccer ball that had bounced out into the street.

"Get that ball out of the street!" the cyclist roared as he sped by T. J.

With a dash and a fast dribble, T. J. rescued the ball and returned to the group of boys on the sidewalk.

"Whew!" T. J.'s best friend, Zack, breathed a sigh of relief. "That was a close call!"

"That motorcycle almost turned you into mush," Anthony told T. J. "Maybe next time you'll listen to me when I tell you it's dumb to pass a soccer ball back and forth so close to the street."

T. J. shrugged his shoulders. Anthony was always trying to boss people around. Of course, he would never pass the ball. Anthony hated to play with balls and was too lazy to play soccer.

With shorter passes and more controlled dribbling, T. J. and Zack continued to move the ball down the sidewalk behind Anthony and the other boys. They were on their way to Anthony's house for a Cub Scout meeting. Anthony's mother, Mrs. Biggins, was their den mother.

T. J. remembered how excited he and Zack had been to join Cub Scouts this past fall when they started second grade. But having Anthony around almost spoiled the whole thing. Just because Anthony's mother was the den mother, Anthony thought he had special privileges and everyone had to do what he said.

"Hey, Jim," Anthony hollered at one of the boys in the group. "Slow down! You can't walk ahead of me. You have to walk behind me."

"Why?" Jim frowned.

"Because we're going to my house, and I'm the leader!" said Anthony. He held out an arm to keep the boys from going around him.

T. J. and Zack grinned at each other and then shot out from behind the group, passing Anthony on either side. They ignored Anthony's angry protests and dribbled the soccer ball at top speed up Juniper Street hill. Reaching the top, the boys plunged down the other side and did not stop until they reached Anthony's house at the bottom of the hill.

"Why, hello, Zack and Timothy," Mrs. Biggins said when she opened the door. T. J. winced. Mrs. Biggins insisted on calling him "Timothy" even though everyone else called him "T. J." Of course, Timothy John Fairbanks, Jr., was his full name, but no one called him that. No one, that is, but Mrs. Biggins.

"I guess you boys hurried over here because you knew I have a special surprise for you," said Anthony's mother with a smile.

T. J. smiled back. He liked Mrs. Biggins even though she called him Timothy. She was nice and baked the most delicious cakes and cookies. The house always smelled like freshly baked goodies. In fact, T. J. thought he smelled something baking in the oven right now.

"Cinnamon rolls!" Mrs. Biggins told T. J. and Zack when she saw them sniffing the air.

When the rest of the boys arrived, Mrs. Biggins told them about the surprise.

"What special Cub Scout event is held every spring—something that we've all been waiting for?" she asked the boys.

They looked at each other and grinned. "The derby!" they shouted.

"That's right," replied Mrs. Biggins. "It's spring and time to work on your Pinewood Derby race cars."

"Hurray!" the boys yelled. Excited voices rang through the house as they discussed their plans for winning the derby.

That night at the dinner table, T. J. asked his father, "Can we go to the store right after dinner?"

"What for?" his father asked as he winked at T. J.'s mother.

"Aw, Dad, you know. I already told you I want to get a Pinewood Derby kit," T. J. reminded his father.

"Really?" his father teased. The truth was that he had heard about nothing else since he had arrived home from work.

"Dad, please?" T. J. pleaded.

"All right," Father smiled. "If it means that much to you, we'll go to the shopping mall tonight."

"YIPPEE!" shouted T. J.

"Can I go too?" cried Charley, T. J.'s six-year-old brother.

"Me too!" hollered four-year-old Megan.

"Maybe we'll all go," said Mother. "I need to get spring nightgowns for the girls."

T. J. sighed and rolled his eyes toward the ceiling. He had hoped that he and his father could go to the store by themselves. Now it looked like he would be stuck with his younger brother and sisters. Oh well, he would go through any amount of torture to get the Pinewood Derby racing kit—even shopping for spring nightgowns!

T. J.'s thoughts were suddenly interrupted when something cool and wet splashed onto his left arm.

"Oh, gross!" T. J. cried in disgust. His two-year-old sister, Elizabeth, had just dumped her bowl full of applesauce on his arm.

"Uh oh," Elizabeth said. When T. J. leaned over to clean off the applesauce, she wiped her sticky fingers in his hair.

"Cut it out, Elizabeth!" T. J. yelled, pushing her dirty fingers away from him.

"No, no, Elizabeth," Mother said. She started to grab the little girl's hands to wash them, but Sergeant, the family dog, was quicker. Being a large German shepherd, Sergeant could easily reach the tray of Elizabeth's high chair. Before Mother could stop him, the big dog licked up the spilled food and each one of Elizabeth's fingers. Elizabeth laughed in delight.

Mother took Elizabeth to the bathroom to wash her hands while T. J. went into the other bathroom to wash his arm and rinse his hair. When he returned, Charley and Megan giggled loudly at him.

"T. J.'s invented a new kind of shampoo," laughed Charley. "It's called Applesauce Lather."

"Very funny," T. J. replied. He tried to keep a straight face, but before long he was laughing right along with his brother and sister.

After dinner the family hurried to the shopping mall. T. J. was the first to get out of the van and the first inside the mall.

"Hurry up," he called to the rest of his family.

They were so slow! Didn't they know how long he had waited to get his very first Pinewood Derby car? He knew exactly what it was going to look like. He had been planning it for months. It was going to be bright, shiny blue and red with yellow racing stripes. The car would be streamlined right down to its wheels. It would weigh a perfect five ounces and would be the fastest car in the derby!

"Come on, come on," T. J. called impatiently. His baby sister, Elizabeth, was causing the delay. She insisted on getting out of her stroller and was running all over the place.

"Why did Elizabeth have to come anyway?" T. J. muttered to himself. "She's ruining the whole night."

Deciding to take matters into his own hands, T. J. hurried back down the mall and stood in front of the two year old.

"Elizabeth," he said, "do you want a pony ride?"

"Yeth!" the little girl answered immediately.

"Okay," T. J. bent over. Father helped Elizabeth climb on top of T. J.'s shoulders.

"WHEEEEE!" Elizabeth giggled with glee as T. J. pranced down the mall. Every time T. J. leaped into the air, Elizabeth laughed even louder.

T. J. headed straight for the store that sold the

Pinewood Derby kits. The rest of the family had to hurry just to keep up with him. Everything was going fine until T. J. passed a giant fountain in the middle of the mall.

Elizabeth suddenly screamed, "WA-TUH!"

"Huh?" T. J. frowned. "What's the matter?"

"She wants to go see the fountain," Charley informed him.

"Oh no," said T. J. "We're not stopping to see any dumb fountains."

"WA-TUH!" Elizabeth screamed and burst into tears. She jerked herself backwards and would have fallen to the floor if T. J. had not thrown his arms behind his head to catch her.

"Elizabeth, quit being a jerk!" T. J. snapped as he lowered his sister to the floor.

"T. J.," said Mother, catching up with them, "it won't hurt anything if we stop at the fountain for a few minutes. You know Elizabeth likes to look at the water."

"But, Mom," T. J. wailed. "I want to get my car."

"We will get your car after we stop at the fountain," Mother said in her no-nonsense voice.

T. J. glanced at his father. Father shrugged as if to say, "I understand, but you'll just have to wait." He patted T. J.'s head.

Mother and a very happy Elizabeth hurried to

the fountain. T. J. stomped along behind them. He was so busy being angry that he did not notice that Charley and Megan had climbed up the outer wall of the fountain to walk around its rim.

"Charley! Megan! Get off of there! You'll fall!" Mother cried. She and Father ran to get the children off the wall.

"T. J.," Mother called over her shoulder, "keep an eye on Elizabeth!"

T. J. turned to look for his baby sister, but he didn't see her anywhere. Then he spotted her. She had already run to the other side of the fountain and was pointing at something in the water. T. J. wondered how she could move so fast.

T. J. started towards his sister and then gasped. Elizabeth had thrown one leg over the smooth marble wall that surrounded the fountain. She was about to leap into the water!

"NO!" T. J. shouted as loud as he could. "STOP, ELIZABETH! YOU CAN'T SWIM!"

2

THE RESCUE

With a mighty leap forward, T. J. grabbed his sister Elizabeth just as the toe of her shoe reached the water. T. J. hauled her back over the wall of the fountain.

"NO, NO, NO!" the little girl screamed in protest.

"Elizabeth!" T. J. exclaimed. "You could have drowned in that water!"

"BABY!" Elizabeth cried and pointed at the water. "BABY DROWN!"

T. J. turned to the water. "Oh no," he wailed. Elizabeth's favorite baby doll—the one that she had to sleep with and take wherever she went— somehow had fallen into the water! The doll floated in slow circles around and around the center of the fountain.

"GET BABY!" Elizabeth looked up at T. J. hopefully, her big blue eyes full of tears.

"Why'd you have to throw her in the water anyway?" T. J. sighed. He was starting to wonder if he'd ever get his racing car kit.

Feeling very frustrated, T. J. stared at the doll bobbing in the water. It was several feet out to the center of the fountain. He did not see how he could get the doll without wading through the fountain, and T. J. knew better than to do that. Besides getting all wet, he just might get electrocuted.

"Excuse me," someone tapped T. J.'s shoulder.

T. J. whirled around and found himself face to face with a boy about his own age.

"My little brother just bought a garden set at the toy store," the boy said. "Maybe you could reach the doll with one of these." He held up a long package containing a plastic rake, a shovel, and a hoe.

Leaning as far out over the water as he dared, T. J. stretched the plastic rake toward the doll. It was no good. The rake missed the doll by several inches.

"Maybe we could hook the tools together," the other boy suggested. "I bet we could hook the end of the rake onto the shovel handle."

"Yeah, let's try it," T. J. agreed.

The boys stuck the prongs of the rake through

the handle of the shovel, trying their best to fasten the tools together.

"Don't break my rake!" the boy's little brother cried when T. J. unsuccessfully tried to twist two prongs together.

"Okay, okay," said T. J. "Well, here goes nothing," he said to the other boy.

Once again T. J. leaned over the fountain wall and stretched out the rake which now had a shovel attached to its end.

By now a rather large crowd of children and adults stood around the fountain to witness the rescue of Elizabeth's baby doll. T. J.'s family had to squeeze through the crowd to reach him.

T. J. had just managed to extend the rake and shovel contraption out far enough across the water to reach the doll when his father's voice suddenly shouted, "T. J.!"

T. J. jumped. The rake and shovel splashed into the water and floated away to join Elizabeth's doll in the center of the fountain.

"Oh no!" T. J. moaned and collapsed to the floor, holding his head in his hands.

"GET MY RAKE AND SHOVEL!" hollered the little brother.

"BABY! WANT BABY!" cried Elizabeth.

T. J.'s father quickly grabbed the other garden

tool, reached out with his long arms, and pulled in the rake and the shovel. He then stretched for the baby doll.

"Got her!" he exclaimed as he held up the dripping doll in triumph.

Everyone clapped at the rescue.

"BABY!" Elizabeth squealed and held out her arms. "OOOOH, BABY WET!" Elizabeth scolded as soon as Father placed the wet doll in her arms. Elizabeth spanked the doll.

T. J., Father, and Elizabeth hurried over to where Mother, Charley, and Megan waited for them. Mother looked at her watch.

"We don't have much more time to shop," she said. "It's getting close to bedtime."

The children groaned at that announcement, and T. J. looked at his father anxiously.

Father quickly handed Mother some money. "You take Charley and the girls over to that little shop for some ice cream," he told her. "T. J. and I have some unfinished business to do."

T. J. grinned with relief. He and his father hurried past the mall shops and into a large department store. They rode the escalator up to the second floor. T. J. knew exactly where to go. He led Father straight to the department that sold the Pinewood Derby kits. He picked out the best looking kit and Father paid for it.

"At last," T. J. sighed to himself. "At last I have my race car."

Visions of a blue and red car with yellow racing stripes sped through his mind. He could hardly wait to get home and start to work on his car.

The next evening, however, T. J. discovered that it was not so easy to make a Pinewood Derby race car.

"I don't think this is going to work, son," Father said.

T. J. sighed and threw his pocket knife down on the table. He stared disgustedly at what was supposed to be the beginning of a fantastic racing car. Instead, the block of wood was a mess. Nicks and gouges covered its surface and there was one rather deep cut where Father had tried to shape the wood with a handsaw.

"What are we going to do?" T. J. frowned.

"I guess I'll call Joe Latham and see how he shapes his cars," Father answered, moving to the telephone.

"Who's Joe Latham?" T. J. asked. He followed Father into the kitchen.

"He's a man at the office. He has two sons that have been in Scouts for years," replied Father. He gave T. J.'s nose a tweak. "Don't worry. If anybody knows how to make derby cars, it's old Joe."

T. J. sat at the kitchen table and listened hopefully to his father's side of the conversation. He wondered how grown-ups learned to talk with so many "uh huhs" and "hmmmmms."

After a while, Father hung up the phone. "I think we have the solution," he said.

"Really?" cried T. J. "What is it?"

"Well, Joe said he always uses a power saw to shape his cars," Father replied.

"A power saw!" T. J. exclaimed. "Where are we going to get a power saw?"

"Well, tomorrow night, right after dinner, you and I will go over to Joe's and use his power saw," answered Father.

"You mean he said we could use it?" T. J. asked as he bounced around the kitchen. "Oh boy!"

The next evening, Father and T. J. drove to Joe Lathams' house. T. J. was glad that his younger brother and sisters did not have to come with them this time. There were certain things an older brother needed to do with his father.

Stepping into Mr. Latham's basement made T. J. really appreciate sharing an adventure with his father. It was fantastic! The smell of freshly sawed wood filled the air. Wood shavings covered the

floor. The walls were filled with rows of screw-drivers, hammers, pliers, and other tools. A long wooden table in the center of the room held what looked like a mountain of machinery. It was, all in all, a perfect place for a boy to explore.

Father introduced T. J. to Joe Latham and to Mr. Latham's son, John. John was four years older than T. J. He was twelve and in the sixth grade.

Mr. Latham seemed to know all there was to know about making Pinewood Derby race cars. He asked T. J. to describe the kind of car he wanted—whether it should be smooth and sleek and shaped for speed or whether it should have all the extras including a fin on the back, a seat for plastic people to sit on, and a place for a windshield.

T. J. thought carefully about it. He finally decided he wanted to make his car as streamlined as possible. He would go for speed.

Very carefully, T. J. drew the shape of his car onto the block of wood. Then Mr. Latham noisily cut the wood according to T. J.'s sketch.

"Here you are, young man," said Mr. Latham as he handed T. J. the cut block of wood.

T. J. gasped in delight. Gone were the ugly nicks and gouges of his pocket knife! Gone was the saw cut made by Father's handsaw! T. J. held in his hands the beginnings of a super fast race car!

"Awesome!" T. J. said.

"That looks pretty good," said Mr. Latham's son, John. "Of course, you'll have to sand it and paint it before it really looks good. Do you want to come up to my room and see my cars? I can show you last year's derby winner."

"Can I, Dad?" T. J. asked excitedly.

T. J.'s father nodded and T. J. and John hurried up to John's bedroom. There, perched on the top of a bookshelf, were several of the most fantastic cars T. J. had ever seen.

"This is the car that won first place last year," John said, picking up a shiny black car with yellow racing stripes. He pointed to a large gold trophy sitting on top of a dresser.

"Wow!" T. J. said.

"I won the design trophy with this car two years ago," said John, pointing to a green, white, and orange car. It had double racing stripes and a big number ten painted on its hood. The tail end of the car swooped up high while the nose dipped towards the ground.

"That is incredible!" T. J. exclaimed when John placed the car in his hands. "I'm gonna put three colors on my car too and a number on the hood. Hey! I have some dynamite dinosaur stickers at home. Do you think I could put one of them on my car?"

"Oh yeah," John replied. "A dinosaur would be fantastic! What kind of dinosaur would you use?"

"It would have to be a Tyrannosaurus rex," T. J. answered without hesitation.

"Why do you want a Tyrannosaurus rex?" John asked.

"Because a Tyrannosaurus rex was strong and powerful. Did you know that it got to be forty feet long and ten feet high? Anyway, it was ferocious. A Tyrannosaurus rex was the most feared meat eater of all the dinosaurs, and that's how I want my race car to be—strong, powerful, and the most feared. I want everyone to be afraid to race against it because it's so fast!" T. J. said proudly.

John smiled at T. J. "I'm sure your car will be absolutely awesome."

"You bet it will!" T. J. agreed. "Just wait and see. I'll have the fastest and neatest looking car in the whole pack!"

3

REVENGE?

"TAKE IT DOWN, T. J.! TAKE IT DOWN! GO ALL THE WAY! GO, T. J., GO!" hollered the boys' soccer coach.

Pushing the ball in front of him, T. J. streaked out in front of the other players and pounded his way down the right side of the soccer field. It was a perfect breakaway and excitement surged through every part of his body.

T. J. heard his coach yell, "CROSS IT! CROSS IT OVER TO ZACK!"

Shoving the ball out in front of him with his left leg, T. J. swung his right leg at the ball, putting all the energy he had into the kick. The ball shot sideways through the air about chest high and landed a foot or so in front of Zack and the goal.

"PERFECT CROSS! PERFECT CROSS!" his coach shouted.

Zack lunged forward to pop the ball into the goal. Unfortunately, the fullback had a different idea. He got in front of the ball so that it hit his legs and bounced out of bounds.

"THAT'S IT FOR THE DAY!" their coach shouted to end practice.

T. J. sighed. He had made such a good run up the field and such a good cross kick. Too bad his friend, Zack, had missed the shot.

"Sorry, T. J.," Zack apologized as soon as he reached his friend.

"Aw, don't worry about it," T. J. put an arm around his friend's shoulders. No one should be mad at his best friend for missing a soccer goal, not when he had tried his best.

"We'll get the goal next time," T. J. told Zack as the boys started to walk home from practice.

"Hey, wait up!" a voice called. "I'll walk with you."

It was Aaron Miller, a classmate and neighbor. T. J. and Zack liked Aaron. He laughed a lot and seemed to always come up with a good joke when one was needed. Aaron was also turning out to be one of the best goalkeepers in the second grade division.

"Great pass, T. J.," Aaron said as soon as he caught up with them. "I guess you're about ready to go professional."

"Thanks," T. J. laughed and then shrugged. "It was no big deal."

"No big deal?" Zack exclaimed. "Are you crazy? It was perfect and I blew it!"

"No, you didn't," T. J. quickly replied. "Your shot was blocked. That's all."

"Yeah," Aaron agreed. "You'll get it next time—no problem!"

The boys walked on. They passed a ball around as they walked.

"Have you guys started work on your Pinewood Derby cars yet?" Aaron asked, changing the subject.

"Sure," T. J. answered. He told Zack and Aaron about his visit to the Lathams' and how Mr. Latham had shaped his car with his power tools.

"Then we had to sand it and drill a couple of holes in the bottom and fill them with lead," T. J. added.

"What for?" his friends asked.

"The car was too light after Mr. Latham shaved all the extra wood off of it, T. J. explained. "You see," he went on, "the race cars should weigh exactly five ounces. They can't be any heavier or they get disqualified and they shouldn't be any lighter or they won't be fast enough to win."

"Oh," his friends nodded their heads.

"My car was a little too light, so we had to fill it with melted lead," T. J. said. "Then we weighed it and it came out just right. Now I'm almost finished with the first sanding, and then I'll get to put on the first coat of paint."

"What do you mean the first coat of paint?" Aaron moaned. "Do we have to paint our cars more than once?"

"Oh yeah," answered T. J. "John Latham said he always gives his cars five or six coats of paint to make them real smooth and shiny."

"Whew!" the other boys whistled.

"I'd better hurry up," Zack decided. "I haven't even started on mine."

"Me neither," said a worried Aaron.

"You'd better get going," T. J. told them. "There are only three more weeks until the big race."

When T. J. got home he went straight to the kitchen. He grabbed a carton of juice and several cookies and started upstairs to his room. Mother stopped him.

"How was soccer practice, T. J.?" she asked.

"Fine," T. J. replied.

"Are you going upstairs to your room?" Mother asked. There was something in the tone of her voice that worried T. J.

"I was going to work on my race car," said T. J. "Why?"

"Uh, about your race car," Mother said slowly.

"Yeah, what about it?" T. J. asked anxiously.

"Well, I think it will be all right . . ." Mother hesitated.

T. J. did not wait to hear any more. He set down the juice and cookies and dashed up the stairs and into his room. He rushed over to the desk where he had been working on his car just the night before.

There it was—the beautifully shaped, aerodynamic race car—covered with Sesame Street® stickers! And that was not all. There were pink crayon designs scribbled around each sticker!

T. J. clenched his fists as he stared at the car. He could feel his face grow hot as the anger boiled inside of him. Who would have done such a thing to his car? Certainly not Charley. T. J. was sure his brother wouldn't have done it. It had to have been his sister Megan. Elizabeth might have helped, but he was sure it had been Megan's idea.

Pounding his fist into his hand, T. J. turned to go find Megan. He would show her what it meant to mess with his Pinewood Derby car. He'd make sure she never touched his car again!

Mother, however, was quicker than T. J. Before

he could run out of his bedroom, she grabbed him.

"Let me go! Let me go!" T. J. hollered.

"I will let you go as soon as you calm down," Mother said gently but firmly. She held onto T. J. until he had calmed down enough to listen to her.

She led him to the bed where they both sat down. Mother put her arm around T. J.'s shoulders.

"I'm sorry about your car, T. J.," Mother said. "I didn't realize what the girls were doing until it was too late."

"So it was Megan?" T. J. asked his mother. He clenched his fists again.

"Yes, and I have already punished Megan and Elizabeth," Mother replied. "I am sure your father will have something to say about it when he gets home."

T. J. shrugged his shoulders. He was too upset to say any more. He was afraid he might start crying.

Just then there was a crash downstairs. Immediately Charley yelled, "Mom!"

Mother jumped off the bed. "Oh dear, I better go see what happened." She patted T. J.'s arm. "Why don't you come downstairs with me."

"No, thanks," T. J. mumbled.

"Okay." Mother walked to the door. "Don't take any of the stickers off your car or erase any

of the crayon marks yet," she said as she turned to leave. "I want your father to see the car just as it is."

After his mother had gone, T. J. did not move from the bed. He just sat for the longest time. He stared at the mess his sisters had made of his car. The more he looked at it, the madder he became. By the time Father got home, T. J. was in an absolute rage.

"Knock, knock," someone called from the doorway of T. J.'s bedroom.

"Come in," T. J. snapped.

"Is it safe?" his father asked. He held his arms

up in front of his face as if he were afraid of being attacked.

T. J. didn't answer. He didn't feel like laughing at his father's joke. Father came into the room. He looked the car over and whistled. "They sure did a job on it, didn't they?" he asked.

"Yeah," T. J. frowned, "and I'd like to . . . !" He slammed his right fist into the palm of his left hand.

"I understand," Father replied, "but you may not hit your sisters. Is that understood?"

"NO!" T. J. shouted. "Why can't I hit them? They came in here and messed up my car. They had no right to do that! They deserve to be clobbered!"

"Maybe they do and maybe they don't," Father said. "That is for me and your mother to decide. We are the parents."

"Parents are lucky," T. J. sulked. "They don't have anyone telling them what to do."

"That's not true," Father told him. "In this case, I will decide the punishment because I am the father of the family and I am responsible for my children's actions. But did you know that I have to answer to a parent too?"

"You do?" T. J. was surprised. "You mean grandpa?"

T. J.'s father laughed. "No, I don't have to answer to grandpa any more. I was talking about God. God is my heavenly Father."

"Oh yeah," T. J. nodded.

"Do you think my heavenly Father would want me to clobber somebody if he messed up my car the way the girls messed up your car?" Father asked T. J.

"I guess not," T. J. answered. It made him smile to imagine the family car covered with Sesame Street® stickers and pink crayon.

"God would not want me to get revenge," Father said. "It says in the Bible that God will take care of our revenge. We're not supposed to get even with someone who hurts us."

"Yeah, I know," T. J. admitted. "But I feel so mad."

T. J.'s father put his arm around T. J.'s shoulders. "Just remember, son," he said gently. "There's always a better way than revenge. Now, let's get those stickers off your car!"

4

GOOEY GLOP!

"Wait 'til you see my car! It's totally awesome! It'll beat any of your cars . . . EASY!" Anthony puffed out his chest and strutted around the playground. It was morning recess and the boys had gathered to discuss the progress of their Pinewood Derby cars.

"Aw, knock it off, Tony-baloney," Zack said to Anthony.

Anthony got mad, but before he could reply Aaron asked T. J., "Did you get all the stickers off your car?"

"Oh yeah," T. J. responded. "It took a lot of soaking and scraping, but my dad and I finally got them off."

"Soaking?" Aaron looked worried. "Did it ruin the wood?"

"Naw, we didn't put the car in water. We used wet sponges to loosen the stickers and then scraped them off with a knife," T. J. explained.

"Boy, your sisters must be really dumb to do something like that to a race car," Anthony sneered at T. J.

T. J. fought the urge to pop Anthony in the nose. He answered, "My sisters are little. They're only two and four years old."

"They still sound dumb to me," jeered Anthony.

T. J. clenched his fists. He took a step towards Anthony.

Zack immediately grabbed T. J. by the arm and turned him away from Anthony. "Come on, T. J. Don't pay attention to dumb old Anthony. He's not worth getting into a fight over."

"That's right," Aaron grabbed T. J.'s other arm. "You might bruise your knuckles on his hard head. Besides, you'd just get in trouble with the teachers."

"NERDY NOSE!" Anthony called after them with an even bigger sneer on his face.

"TONY-BALONEY!" Zack hollered back at him. Zack stuck out his stomach and puffed up his cheeks. He looked so funny that he soon had T. J. and Aaron rolling on the ground, laughing so hard that their sides hurt.

"Whew!" T. J. finally stood up. He gave Zack a playful punch on the shoulder. "Thanks for keeping me out of a fight with Anthony. If I could just stay away from him everything would be fine."

"No problem," said Zack. "That's what friends are for!"

"Hey, let's go kick around the soccer ball," Aaron suggested. "That's also what friends are for."

The three boys hurried off to the soccer field.

"How about a little ketchup on your mashed potatoes?" Zack asked T. J.

It was lunch time and T. J. was busy combining all of the leftover food from his and his friends' trays into one big sloppy mess. He had mixed together coleslaw, mashed potatoes, two packets of butter, and some roast beef gravy. He squirted the packet of ketchup on top of the gooey mixture.

"Here's something else," said Aaron. He took a carrot stick from another boy's lunch and stuck it upright in the slop on T. J.'s tray.

"Awesome!" the boys exclaimed. The carrot looked like an empty flag pole surrounded by a sea of sticky lava.

"You better throw that out before Mrs. Hubbard sees it," Anthony warned, as he poked his face over T. J.'s shoulder. Mrs. Hubbard was their second grade teacher. If she caught anyone mixing food, she would make that person eat the whole mess.

"Shut up, Anthony," the boys replied.

Anthony glared at the other boys and held his hand high in the air. "Mrs. Hubbard!" he yelled, trying to get the teacher's attention.

"Cut it out, Anthony!" T. J. hissed over his shoulder. He looked at Zack and Aaron. Panic was written all over his face. He did not want to have to eat the gloppy mess on his tray! "What should I do, Zack?"

"Your milk carton!" Zack cried. "Quick, shove it all into your milk carton!"

T. J. gulped down the last of his milk, and he and Zack began spooning the runny mixture of food into the empty carton.

"Mrs. Hubbard is on her way!" Aaron warned them.

The boys went as fast as they could, but it was not easy to spoon the slop into the small opening in the milk carton. T. J. felt his muscles tense and his face grow hot. He could hear Anthony laughing. Anthony was going to get it! Somehow, he was going to pay for this!

Just as Mrs. Hubbard reached the table, T. J. spooned the last of the slop into the milk carton. He quickly closed the opening.

"What seems to be the problem, boys?" Mrs. Hubbard asked, coming up right behind T. J.

"Oh, uh, nothing, Mrs. Hubbard," Zack answered the teacher.

"Why did you call me over, Anthony?" the teacher asked.

The boys glared at Anthony. There was a moment of anxious silence. Finally Anthony shrugged and said, "Oh, never mind. Everything's okay now."

The teacher looked at Anthony for a moment, then turned and walked away.

"WHEW!" T. J., Zack, and Aaron breathed heavy sighs of relief. They glared at Anthony as he went back to his own table.

"I'm gonna get even with him if it's the last thing I do," T. J. vowed.

"Anthony has gone too far this time," declared Aaron.

"I agree," said Zack, "and I've got a great idea how to pay him back. What would you say to sharing a little of our gooey glop with Anthony?" Zack patted the milk carton on T. J.'s tray.

"Yeah!" the boys answered.

"Okay, what we'll do is . . ." Zack motioned the boys to pull their chairs closer together and told them his plan.

"It's perfect, just perfect!" T. J. exclaimed.

That afternoon at recess, T. J., Zack, and Aaron waited until Mrs. Hubbard was at the far end of the playground. They scurried around the side of the school building to the open window of their classroom.

"Quick! Boost me up!" said T. J.

Zack and Aaron each grabbed one of T. J.'s legs and hoisted him up to the window ledge. T. J. pushed on the window screen. It opened easily.

T. J. climbed through the window and jumped to the classroom floor. His heart was pounding so hard that he thought for sure someone would hear it. He ran to his desk and pulled out the milk carton that was hidden inside.

T. J. tiptoed to Anthony's desk, trying not to spill the carton. He rummaged through the desk until he found Anthony's math workbook. T. J. pulled it out and turned to the assignment that was due that afternoon.

Taking a deep breath, T. J. poured the slop from the milk carton onto the workbook page. He closed the book carefully and set it back inside Anthony's desk.

T. J. ran to the window and climbed back outside. He pulled the window screen back into place before leaping to the ground. After hiding the milk carton behind a bush, he turned and grinned at his friends.

"Did you do it?" Zack and Aaron asked excitedly.

"Of course!" T. J. replied.

"Awesome!" both boys cheered, obviously impressed by their friend's courage.

"Come on, we better get out of here," said Zack.

The boys raced to the end of the building and peeked around the corner.

"Oh no," T. J. whispered. "There's Mrs. Hubbard!"

True enough, Mrs. Hubbard stood with her back to the boys not more than twenty feet away. There was no way to slip around her to get back to the playground where they belonged.

"If we get caught over here, we're in big trouble," Aaron worried.

"Shhhhh," Zack held his finger to his lips. "We'll figure something out."

The boys waited and waited. Why didn't Mrs. Hubbard move? What if the bell rang to go inside? They would surely be seen coming from the wrong side of the building. Then when Anthony's workbook was discovered, everyone would know that they had done it.

Just when the boys thought they could wait no longer, a scream from the other side of the playground sent Mrs. Hubbard running. Someone had fallen off the swing set and needed help.

T. J., Zack, and Aaron sneaked around the corner of the building back to the playground. A few seconds later, the bell rang. The boys lined up with the other children to go back to their classroom.

Sitting down at their own desks, T. J., Zack, and Aaron tried to look as innocent as possible. Out of the corners of their eyes, they watched Anthony's every move.

As usual, Anthony was the last one back in the classroom. Mrs. Hubbard had to ask him several times to take his seat. When he did sit down, he did not open his desk but sat and whispered to the boy beside him.

T. J. could hardly stand it. When was Anthony going to open his desk? What would he say when he saw his math workbook? What would Mrs. Hubbard say?

T. J. slumped in his chair. If Mrs. Hubbard found out that he was the one who put the glop in Anthony's workbook, he would get into a lot of trouble. Surely Anthony wouldn't tell on him, would he?

"It's time to go over our math lesson," Mrs. Hubbard announced. "Please take out your math workbooks."

Immediately, T. J. sat up in his chair. He stared at Anthony. How bad would his workbook look? Would the goop run out quickly or just ooze out around the corners?

"Oooooooooh! Disgusting!" Anthony suddenly screamed. He jerked his math workbook out of his desk. A greenish-brown liquid ran over the desk and onto the floor.

"Oh gross!" his classmates yelled.

"What is it?" cried Mrs. Hubbard.

Anthony dropped the workbook onto the floor where it oozed into a squishy puddle of slop. Everyone around him held their noses as the stink began to fill the room.

Some of the children began to laugh, and cries of "Tony-baloney" filled the air. T. J. was laughing so hard that he could hardly sit in his chair.

Mrs. Hubbard stood at the front of the room and clapped her hands for attention. "Who is responsible for this?" she asked.

A complete silence fell across the room. T. J. held his breath. He could feel his face grow hot.

"I know who did it!" Anthony cried all of a sudden. "I know exactly who did it!"

All eyes turned to Anthony. His face was purple and his body shook with rage. He stood up and pointed his finger. "IT WAS T. J.!" he shouted.

5

TROUBLE!

T. J. cringed and slid down into his chair. He glanced at his teacher, Mrs. Hubbard. She did not seem a bit happy.

Anthony continued to point his finger. "T. J. DID IT! T. J. DID IT!" he hollered again and again.

"Anthony, please stop shouting and sit down," Mrs. Hubbard ordered. She was holding one hand to her forehead as if her head ached. "T. J., come out in the hallway at once."

T. J. got up and slowly followed his teacher out the door. His classmates giggled and a few cheered as he passed their desks.

"T. J., I can't believe it was you!" Mrs. Hubbard said as soon as she and T. J. were alone. "What in the world made you do such a thing?"

"I dunno," T. J. replied in a low voice. He hung his head and would not look at his teacher.

"What do you mean you don't know?" Mrs. Hubbard threw her hands in the air. "People don't go around filling other people's math books with slimy goop for no reason at all!"

T. J. squirmed as Mrs. Hubbard stared at him and finally mumbled, "I guess I did it because Anthony has been such a jerk lately."

"Tell me about it," said Mrs. Hubbard.

Once he got going, T. J. found it easy to give Mrs. Hubbard a whole list of reasons why he damaged Anthony's math workbook. He told her how Anthony always had to be the boss and how he picked on T. J. and made fun of his soccer playing. He also told her how Anthony had called his sisters dumb and how he had tried to get him in trouble at lunchtime when T. J. had mixed the slop together on his tray.

Mrs. Hubbard smiled and put one hand on T. J.'s shoulder. "Maybe it would have been better if I had made you eat that goop," she said. "You wouldn't be in trouble now."

"Yeah," T. J. sighed.

"I understand why you were angry with Anthony," Mrs. Hubbard said, "but destroying his math book was wrong. I'm afraid you'll have to go see Mrs. Larson."

T. J. gulped. Mrs. Larson was Kingswood

Elementary School's principal. Going to see the principal because you had done something wrong was not a fun thing to do. However, before Mrs. Hubbard and T. J. could begin their walk to Mrs. Larson's office, the classroom door suddenly opened and out came Zack and Aaron.

"We couldn't let T. J. take the blame by himself," Zack told Mrs. Hubbard.

"You mean you boys were in on it too?" their teacher asked.

Zack and Aaron nodded.

"Then all three of you had better come with me to see Mrs. Larson," said Mrs. Hubbard.

T. J. smiled gratefully at Zack and Aaron. He was glad to have such loyal friends. It would be much less scary to go to the principal's office with his friends.

The three boys followed their teacher down the hall to the school office. Mrs. Hubbard disappeared into the principal's private office and left the boys waiting with the school secretary.

T. J. fidgeted uneasily. He knew Mrs. Larson would not be happy. She was a nice lady, but she could be very stern when children misbehaved. He wished the door to Mrs. Larson's office would never open.

It wasn't long before the door did open and

out came Mrs. Hubbard. "You may go in now," she told the boys.

When the boys got inside, Mrs. Larson pointed to some chairs for them to sit on. She looked long and hard at each one of them in turn.

T. J. could not return the principal's stare. He felt like Mrs. Larson's eyes were drilling a hole through his forehead and reading the jumble of thoughts and feelings inside. He quickly lowered his eyes to the floor.

"You boys have committed a serious offense," Mrs. Larson finally spoke. "You have destroyed school property!"

T. J. swallowed hard. He had not meant to destroy school property. He had only meant to get back at Anthony for trying to get him in trouble at lunchtime.

"T. J.," Mrs. Larson looked directly at him. "I would like to hear why you put garbage inside a math workbook."

T. J. tried to sit as straight as he could. His mouth went dry. Awkwardly, he tried to explain to Mrs. Larson why he had been so mad at Anthony. But somehow nothing that he said seemed to be a good enough reason to destroy school property.

Mrs. Larson listened carefully to T. J. and then questioned Zack and Aaron.

"I understand your problems with Anthony," she told the boys when they had finished speaking. "However, destroying Anthony's math book was not the answer. By doing that, you behaved just as badly as he did. Getting revenge never helps. It only adds to the problem."

T. J. sighed to himself. Mrs. Larson sounded just like his father. She was saying the same things he'd said the night before. *Why couldn't I have listened to him, even for one day?* T. J. thought. *He'll be so disappointed that I gave in and tried to get revenge. I hope he doesn't find out.*

T. J.'s hope was immediately dashed. "I am going to have to put you boys into detention for one week," said Mrs. Larson, "and I'm going to have to call your parents."

That night, T. J. spent a long and lonely evening in his room. He didn't feel like doing anything. He and his dog, Sergeant, sat on the edge of his bed. T. J. thought about the events of the day.

He wished he had never put the slop from his tray into Anthony's math workbook. That had been really stupid. Now he was in trouble with everyone, including his parents.

"T. J., how could you have done such a thing?"

his mother had exclaimed when she heard the news.

"T. J., I'm very disappointed with what you've done," his father had told him.

T. J. kicked his desk chair angrily. He was stuck all alone in his room, and he felt miserable. And it was only the first of seven such nights! He was grounded for a whole week and could not even go to soccer practice!

"STUPID! STUPID! STUPID!" T. J. yelled at himself. He kicked his wastebasket as hard as he could. The metal can flew across the room and banged into the closet door. A trail of trash littered the room.

After T. J. calmed down a bit, he picked up the trash and the wastebasket. He decided he might as well work on his race car since there wasn't much else he could do. He got out the shiny blue enamel paint his father had bought for him and started to work.

By bedtime, T. J. had put the first coat of paint on his race car. This accomplishment made him feel much better. At least if he had to stay in his room every night, he would get his car painted.

And that's just what he did. Every day after school T. J. lightly sanded his car, and then after dinner he gave it a fresh coat of paint. By Friday evening he had given his car five coats of paint. Its rich blue color gleamed brightly under the light on his desk.

"You've done a good job, son," praised his father. "What more do you have left to do on your car?"

"I'm going to put the stripes and the dinosaur sticker on tomorrow," T. J. answered, "and then the only thing left to do is put on the wheels."

"Very good," Father nodded. "I better help you with the wheels. I've heard they can be pretty tricky to get on."

"Thanks, Dad," T. J. grinned. He and Father had become extra close this past week. While T. J. was grounded, they had had several long talks. T. J. was truly sorry for what he had done to Anthony's math workbook. He had prayed to God for forgiveness.

T. J. was up early on Saturday. He couldn't wait to decorate his car. He had been waiting for this part for a long time.

With pieces of scotch tape, T. J. carefully marked two long diagonal stripes on each side of his car. Taking a tiny watercolor brush, he filled in both stripes with bright yellow paint. He then painted a yellow rectangular area on the hood of the car. On the roof he painted a large light blue triangle and painted the number five inside of it. He then added two more stripes on the upper sides of the car. He painted those shiny red. Finally, after everything was painted and dry, T. J. carefully put a Tyrannosaurus rex sticker in the middle of the yellow rectangle on the hood of his car.

T. J. pushed his chair back and studied his race car. His face broke into a grin. It was absolutely awesome, just as John Latham had said it would be. It was every bit as good looking as one of John's cars, and it had to be every bit as fast. At least it would be if T. J. and his father could fasten the wheels on right. Where was his father? Maybe he was ready to help with the wheels.

T. J. found his father outside in the backyard. He was busy starting the lawn mower.

"Wait until I finish mowing the lawn and then we'll put on the wheels!" his father shouted above the roar of the mower.

T. J. stomped back into the house. It would take his father forever to mow the lawn! He couldn't wait that long. He wanted to finish his car, now!

The television was on, so T. J. plopped himself

down in front of it and tried to watch cartoons with Charley and Megan, but he couldn't think about anything except his race car. If he could just get the wheels on, it would be finished. Then he wouldn't have to worry about it anymore.

T. J. headed back upstairs and got out the box that used to hold all of his car parts. The only things left in the box were four wheels and four nails. Maybe he should try putting the wheels on by himself. After all, how hard could it be?

T. J. picked up one of the tiny nails and slid it through a wheel. He tried to fit it into a slit on the bottom of his car, but it wouldn't go in all the way. T. J. used the top of a small screwdriver to hammer the nail and wheel into place. The nail acted as a miniature axle.

Using the same method, T. J. hammered the other wheels into place. Then, holding a tube of super glue over each axle, he squeezed out a drop and fastened the axles securely into the bottom slits of the car.

Everything seemed all right until T. J. turned the car right-side-up and set it on its wheels. He then discovered that one of the wheels was shorter than the others. One would not turn at all. A drop of glue had accidentally landed on part of the wheel and had glued it to the axle. The wheel was permanently frozen!

"Oh no!" T. J. wailed and sank down in his chair. He covered his face with his hands and moaned. His car couldn't race now! He had ruined it! His beautiful, awesome, fantastic car—ruined!

T. J. moaned as he rested his head in his hands. "Dad told me to wait to put on the wheels until he'd finished mowing the lawn. What am I going to do?"

6

THE DERBY!

T. J. sat upstairs in his bedroom and stared at his race car for the longest time. Sergeant came into his room and laid his head in T. J.'s lap. The dog always seemed to know when T. J. was upset. Petting the dog's head, T. J. waited for the lawn mower to stop. He dreaded telling his father that he had ruined his car because he'd tried to put on the wheels himself, especially when Father had asked him to wait for his help.

The lawn mower stopped. T. J. dragged his way downstairs. He found Father in the garage putting away the mower.

"You did what?" Father exclaimed when he heard T. J.'s sad story. He immediately followed T. J. upstairs to inspect the damage.

"Well, I'm afraid you are right. I think the wheels are ruined," Father said, holding up the car and peering at its underside. He tried to move a wheel. It wouldn't budge.

"Let me see if I can get the wheels off," sighed Father. He got a pair of needle-nose pliers and pulled and yanked and pulled until he was finally able to get all the wheels off the car.

"They're totally destroyed," T. J. sighed as he inspected the dented and mangled wheels lying on his desk.

Father nodded his head. "I wish you had waited for me to help you put on the wheels."

"I'm sorry," T. J. apologized.

"The next time I tell you to do something, I want you to do it," replied Father firmly. He left the room. In a few minutes, he returned and said, "I guess I could go to the store and buy another kit to get a new set of wheels."

"Oh, would you?" T. J. jumped up in relief. "Can I go with you?"

"No," Father said. "You're still grounded, remember? I want you to stay here and think about what you've done and how you could have obeyed me."

While his father was gone, T. J. had plenty of time to think. His father was right. He should have listened to him and not tried to put on the wheels himself. It was like the other day when he should have obeyed his father and not taken revenge on Anthony. Everything his father had asked him to do was for his own good. When would he learn to listen?

T. J. waited and waited for his father to return. What was taking him so long? Father was so late that Mother called the rest of the family to lunch without him.

T. J. could not stop worrying. What if the store had sold out of Pinewood Derby kits? What if Father could not find one?

Finally his father's car pulled into the driveway. T. J. ran to the front door.

"I think I got the very last Pinewood Derby kit in the city," Father said as he dragged into the house. "I had to go to three different stores!"

He handed T. J. the package. T. J. eagerly tore open the kit. He counted the wheels and nails. There were four each.

"Whew!" he sighed in relief.

"We can't mess up on the wheels this time," Father warned. After Father ate lunch, he and T. J. went upstairs.

"Joe Latham said that the wheels can't be too close to the bottom of the car," Father explained, "or they will rub on the bottom. But they can't be too far away from the bottom of the car, or they will wobble."

T. J. and his father worked together to attach the wheels to the nails, then Father pulled the nails through the slits on the bottom of the car with the needle-nose pliers. After all the nails were pulled through the slits, Father set the car right-side-up on its wheels.

"Not too bad," he said, stroking his chin, "but I think the right front wheel might be a little higher than the others." Father and T. J. fiddled with the wheel, lowering it ever so slightly.

"Now I think the back left one is too high," T. J. frowned.

"Do you think so?" Father studied the car. He got on his knees and scrunched down to get eye level with the top of the desk.

Father and T. J. fiddled and fiddled with the wheels. They raised and lowered all of them, checking for rub and wobble.

By late afternoon they decided they'd had enough. The wheels were as perfect as they could get them. Holding their breath, they glued the axles into place.

After the glue had dried, T. J. checked the wheels. They all turned freely. There was no rub and there was no wobble. Father got out a long plank of wood and he and T. J. raced the car down the plank many times.

T. J.'s eyes sparkled with excitement. He grinned from ear to ear. He couldn't wait until his friends saw this car! He was going to beat them all! He was sure that this would be the fastest car in the Pinewood Derby!

All the next week, T. J. helped Zack and Aaron finish their cars. Like T. J., Zack had built his car for speed, but Aaron had decided to go for design. His shiny black and yellow car had a plastic windshield and an entire family of plastic people sitting on his customized seats.

"You will definitely win the design trophy Friday night," Zack told Aaron as he and T. J. watched Aaron put the finishing touches on his car.

"Maybe so," Aaron shrugged. He acted as if he didn't care, but T. J. knew it would mean a lot to Aaron if he won the trophy for the best design. It would also mean a lot to T. J. if he won the trophy for the fastest car. He could hardly wait for Friday night. That was when all the dens in Pack Sixteen would meet at Kingswood Elementary School for the big race.

On Friday morning, T. J. was out of bed before anyone else in the family was up. He was dressed and downstairs before his mother had even started the coffee.

"I haven't seen you downstairs this early in the morning in a long time," his mother teased T. J. "For your reward, you may help me set the breakfast table."

T. J. didn't mind setting the table this time. It helped him take his mind off the race that night. How was he ever going to make it through a whole day of waiting?

"This is worse than waiting for Christmas," T. J. told Zack when he got to school.

"Yeah," Zack agreed. "At least on Christmas you know you are going to get something good. But you don't know what's going to happen at the derby!"

Just as T. J. had suspected, the day was horribly slow. Anthony bragged about his car all day, which made it even worse.

"You might as well give up now," Anthony told the other boys. "My car is going to win the trophy."

"I almost wish somebody would drop a ton of bricks on his car," snapped T. J. He was tired of hearing Anthony's boasts.

Finally, long after T. J. thought the day should have ended, the last school bell rang. T. J. rushed home, put on his Cub Scout uniform, and impatiently waited for dinner. When they'd finally finished eating, he and his family piled into the van and headed for the school.

T. J. sat in the back of the van and wiggled with excitement. This was it! The night of the Pinewood Derby was here at last!

The lights of the school building blazed against the dark sky. T. J. and his family joined the other families as they all hurried through the front doors.

Clutching his race car protectively against his chest, T. J. looked for Zack and Aaron. He smiled when he saw a banner hanging above the gymnasium doors. It read "PACK SIXTEEN PINEWOOD DERBY."

Suddenly T. J. heard familiar voices. Zack and Aaron ran to meet him.

"This is fantastic!" T. J. exclaimed, looking around at all the activity in the gym.

"Oh yeah, they have the race tracks already set up," Zack told him excitedly. "Come on, we gotta go weigh in our cars."

"Where do we do that?" T. J. asked.

"Over there," Zack pointed.

In one corner of the gym stood a table that held a set of scales. A line of boys waited behind the table. Anthony's mother, Mrs. Biggins, was busy weighing each boy's race car.

"Come on, Dad," T. J. grabbed his father's arm. "We gotta go weigh in."

Aaron, Zack, T. J., and Father joined the line at the table. Anthony stood right in front of them waiting for his turn.

"See the biggest trophy up there?" Anthony asked the boys, pointing a finger at the winner's table. "I'm gonna win that tonight!"

T. J. stared at the table full of gleaming trophies and brightly colored ribbons. Among them was a trophy more magnificent than all the rest. It was very large and at its top was a shiny brass model of a Pinewood Derby car.

"No way are you going to win that trophy, Tony-baloney," Zack told Anthony.

"I will so!" Anthony shouted and pushed Zack hard.

"Hey! That's enough pushing," Father stepped in. He caught Zack before he crashed into Aaron.

The line moved quickly and soon it was Anthony's turn to weigh in his car. He handed it to his mother who placed it on the scales.

"Five and one-eighth ounces," she read the scales. "You may now get in line to race your car." She handed Anthony his car and pointed him towards several lines of boys waiting in front of the giant wooden race tracks.

"Wait a minute," T. J. heard his father say. Father went over to the weigh-in table. "It says in the rules that the cars are not supposed to weigh more than five ounces," he told Anthony's mother. "I just heard you say that your son's car weighs five and one-eighth ounces."

"I know," Anthony's mother replied, "but we decided not to be so strict on weight."

"But that's not fair," Father argued. "We worked hard to get our car to weigh exactly five ounces. I'm sure other boys did too. If you let in cars that weigh more than five ounces they will win easily."

"Well, let's ask the scoutmaster what he thinks,"

Mrs. Biggins sighed as if she thought Father was making a big deal over nothing.

Anthony's father, Mr. Biggins, was the scoutmaster for Pack Sixteen. Mr. Biggins listened impatiently to Father's complaint.

"Now, Tim," Mr. Biggins called Father by his first name. "We didn't want to be too rigid about the weight of the cars. It's hard enough to make these cars without having to get them to weigh precisely five ounces."

T. J.'s father raised his eyebrows in surprise at such a remark. "The limit is five ounces," he said. "How do you expect to have a fair race if you allow cars to weigh more than the limit?"

"Anthony's car only weighed an eighth of an ounce more than the limit," Mr. Biggins snapped. "That should not make any difference." Without listening to Father's reply, the scoutmaster stomped back to the race track.

"This is not right," Father grumbled as he got back in line beside T. J.

When it was T. J.'s turn to have his car weighed, he handed it proudly to Mrs. Biggins. She placed it on the scales. It weighed exactly five ounces, no more, no less. Mrs. Biggins looked uncomfortably at Father before she sent T. J. over to the race tracks.

As soon as T. J. saw the tracks, he forgot all about the weight of Anthony's car. The tracks were absolutely incredible! Eight starting gates stood above eight lanes of track. A lever at the top of the tracks controlled the opening and closing of the gates. When the scoutmaster raised the lever, individual pins held eight race cars in their gates. But when he lowered the lever, the cars were released all at the same time.

T. J. could not take his eyes off the tracks. It wouldn't be long until his car was at the gates, ready to run in its first Pinewood Derby!

7

CHEATING

T. J. watched anxiously as eight cars were loaded onto the race tracks. Anthony's car was in this race. It was in gate number eight. T. J., Zack, and Aaron were not in this race. They had to wait for the next one.

Anthony's car sat waiting in gate number eight. T. J. wondered if an extra eighth of an ounce would really make a difference in the race. He hoped not. It would be awful if Anthony won the races because his car was too heavy.

"Five, four, three, two, one!" The start of the first race pulled T. J. from his thoughts. The lever was released. The cars shot out of the gates and whizzed down the tracks. The Pinewood Derby had begun!

"GO!" T. J. heard himself yell. He was rooting for all of them—all except Anthony's bright orange car. But almost before T. J. had time to blink, the race was over. Anthony had won.

T. J. turned to look at his father. A big frown covered Father's face. Anthony yelled and screamed in triumph. He went to stand in the winner's area. That was where boys whose cars placed first and second waited. When the first round of races was finished, all the winners of those races would race each other to see who would be the over-all champions and win the first, second, and third place trophies.

It was T. J.'s turn to race. He swallowed hard, stepped up to the track, and carefully placed his car in gate number three. Aaron and Zack were beside him in gates number one and two. T. J. nervously glanced at his father. Father held his thumb in the air and gave T. J. a victory sign.

"Please, Lord . . . " was all T. J. could manage to pray.

"Five, four, three, two, one," rang the countdown. The gates were opened and the race began.

"GO NUMBER FIVE!" T. J. heard his father shout. T. J. could not say a word. He was so tense, he didn't even breathe!

"WINNER—NUMBER FIVE!" the scoutmaster called out. T. J. could hardly believe his ears. He had won! His father grinned from ear to ear.

"RUNNER-UP—NUMBER EIGHT!" announced Mr. Biggins.

T. J. grinned at his best friend. Number eight was Zack's car. He had come in second behind T. J.

A ripple of laughter broke from the audience. A red parachute had burst open at the back of Aaron's car. It had slowed the black and yellow car to a rolling stop at the bottom of the track. The crowd cheered.

"Well, that's my first and last race," Aaron told his friends. "My parachute won't open again."

T. J. and Zack chuckled as their friend gathered up his car and parachute and hustled off to the display table for the design competition.

T. J. was glad that Zack was with him as he stood behind Anthony in the winner's area. It made putting up with Anthony much easier.

"I told you I was going to win," Anthony bragged to T. J. and Zack.

"You haven't won yet, Tony-baloney," snarled Zack.

"Yeah, and if you do win, it'll be because you cheated," T. J. added.

"It will not!" Anthony yelled.

"It will so!" T. J. replied. "Your car is an eighth of an ounce too heavy."

"My dad says that's okay," Anthony retorted.

"Well, he's going against the rules and that's wrong," answered T. J.

"The scoutmaster gets to make up the rules," Anthony declared, "and my dad is the scoutmaster."

"So what?" frowned T. J. "It's still cheating!"

Before Anthony could reply, the first winner's race was called. Anthony's car was in that race and won. T. J. and Zack raced in the next winner's race, and again took first and second.

More races were run, but T. J. and Anthony did not race against each other until the last race. Zack's car was eliminated in the next to the last race. The final eight cars were called for the last race to see which one would win the Pinewood Derby.

T. J. stood beside the race track and tried to keep his hands from shaking as he waited for the race to start. He licked his lips nervously. Both Anthony and T. J. had won all of their separate races. Now they were racing each other.

T. J. glanced at his father. He thought he knew what Father was thinking. If Anthony won the race, it would be because his car was heavier than T. J.'s. It would be because he had cheated.

"Five, four, three, two, one!" the countdown was called. The gates opened and the cars shot forward. The race was on!

"COME ON, NUMBER FIVE!" T. J.'s father yelled.

"GO, NUMBER TWO!" someone else cried.

"HURRY UP, NUMBER FOURTEEN!" called another.

"GO! GO! GO!" T. J. heard himself holler. His car was out in front, neck to neck with Anthony's car. It looked like it might be a tie but at the very bottom of the track, right before it crossed the finish line, Anthony's car nosed a tiny bit in front of T. J.'s.

"WINNER! NUMBER NINE!" the scoutmaster called out Anthony's number.

T. J. could hardly believe his ears. He stood and stared down at the finish line. Had he really lost the race? Had his beautiful blue aerodynamic race car been beaten by Anthony's ugly orange car—the car that should have been disqualified because it was too heavy?

Suddenly, the hurt and disappointment were too much for T. J. to bear. He grabbed his race car and ran out of the gym.

T. J. could not stop the angry tears that ran from his eyes. He had a lump in his throat so big that he had to gasp for breath.

"T. J., are you all right?" his father's voice called out from behind him.

T. J. did not answer. He stumbled blindly down a hallway until strong arms grasped his shoulders and lifted him into the air.

T. J. resisted, but only for a moment. He buried his face in his Father's arms and let the sobs shake his body until he could cry no more. Slowly, the tears stopped.

"It's not fair!" T. J. finally spoke. "I would have won if he hadn't cheated." His voice cracked and his throat ached.

"I agree," Father nodded. He wiped T. J.'s wet face with his handkerchief.

"Can't we do something about it?" T. J. sputtered.

"I already protested about the weight of

Anthony's car," Father reminded him. "It didn't do any good."

"But that's not right!" T. J. cried. "They should go by the rules, and the rules say the cars cannot be heavier than five ounces."

"I know," Father replied, "but there is nothing we can do about it." He looked into T. J.'s eyes. "Life is full of unfair things, T. J. What makes the difference is how you choose to handle them."

"I'd like to handle this one by punching Anthony right in the nose!" T. J. declared.

"Well, I would like to think that by now you have learned that revenge does not solve anything," said Father.

"Yeah, I guess so," T. J. sighed and looked down at the floor.

"Listen, son," Father said gently. "Whenever you look at your race car, you'll have the satisfaction of knowing that you were in the right. But whenever Anthony looks at his race car, he'll know that he had to cheat to win."

T. J. nodded. He knew that what Father said was true.

"Let's wait and let God handle the problem this time," Father suggested. "He has a way of making everything turn out right."

"Okay," T. J. agreed. He did feel a little better.

His eyes were dry and the lump in his throat was gone.

"Come on," Father led T. J. back to the gym. "Getting second place in the Pinewood Derby is a good accomplishment. Let's go collect the trophy."

Back in the gym, T. J. watched as various boys were called to the winner's table to collect ribbons and trophies. He cheered loudly when his friend Aaron got the first place trophy for the most original design. Then, to T. J.'s great surprise, he won a first place trophy for the shiniest paint job! He grinned at his father. All those hours of sanding and painting had paid off.

Finally, it was time to give away the trophies for the fastest cars in the derby. T. J. got a thunderous applause when he went up to get the second place trophy. The tips of his ears turned red as his friends whistled and stomped their feet. He carried his trophy proudly as he went back to his chair. His father was right. Getting second place in the Pinewood Derby was no small matter.

When Anthony went up to receive the first place trophy, however, things went quite a bit differently. A few people clapped politely. No one cheered or whistled. For the most part, the room was silent. Anthony quickly returned to his seat. His face was red with embarrassment. Anthony's father, the scoutmaster, ended the ceremonies quickly.

"Wasn't it strange that hardly anyone clapped for Anthony?" T. J. asked his father as soon as they got to the van.

"I don't think so," Father replied as he turned on the engine and backed out of the parking lot. "Everyone knew that Anthony had won by cheating."

"And everyone knew that you should have won the first place trophy," Mother added.

"Yeah," T. J. thought for a moment, "but I think I got the best deal at the derby."

"What do you mean?" his parents asked.

"Well, I got two trophies, a first place and a second place, and I got the loudest applause of them all," T. J. replied. "You can't beat that!"

"You're right," Father chuckled. "You can't beat that."

8

ANOTHER CHANCE

When T. J. arrived at school Monday morning, the first person he saw was Anthony. He was carrying his Pinewood Derby trophy into the classroom. A crowd of children quickly surrounded Anthony's desk to admire the trophy.

"You oughta go tell everyone how he cheated," Zack urged T. J.

"Yeah, and how you should really be the winner," added Aaron.

"No," T. J. shook his head. "My dad and I had a long talk this weekend, and we decided that I should not get revenge on Anthony for what he did at the derby. I'm going to let God handle this one."

His friends looked surprised but did not argue. They all quietly took their seats.

By lunch time, the truth about the illegal weight of Anthony's Pinewood Derby car had spread so that the whole class knew. T. J. had not said a word about it. Neither had Zack nor Aaron. Perhaps it had been one of the other boys in the pack that had set the class straight.

At recess the children chanted, "Tony-baloney is a phony!" over and over again. It wasn't long before children from other classes picked up the chant. The chant got so loud that it was deafening.

"Do you think God is handling the problem for you?" Zack asked T. J.

"It sure seems like it," T. J. agreed.

"Yeah, I bet old Anthony is sorry he ever brought that trophy to school," laughed Aaron.

The boys watched as Anthony ran as fast as he could across the playground, trying to get away from the crowd of children that chased behind him, still calling out their chant.

After recess Anthony hid his trophy in the coat closet. At the end of the day, he wrapped it in his jacket to carry it home.

That evening at the dinner table T. J. told his family about Anthony and the trophy.

"I didn't say a word about Anthony cheating at the derby," T. J. said, "but somehow, everybody learned about it anyway."

"The truth always gets out," Father replied.

"That's right," Mother nodded. "I hope Anthony

has learned that cheating never makes you a winner."

Just then the telephone rang. Father got up to answer it. After he had listened for a few minutes, he boomed, "Why yes, I think my son would be delighted to get another chance to race his car."

T. J. dropped his fork on his plate with a clatter and looked at Mother in surprise.

"Yes, we'll be at the Kingswood Shopping Mall next Saturday morning at nine o'clock sharp. Thank you for calling." Father hung up the telephone.

"What's going on?" Mother and T. J. asked at once.

Father smiled. "That was your scoutmaster," he said. "It seems that this Saturday there is going to be a county-wide Pinewood Derby race held at the mall. Boys from all over the county will participate. Packs can send their top two boys and their cars to the race."

"Does that mean that I get to go?" T. J. asked excitedly.

"Yes," Father replied, "you and Anthony."

"Anthony!" T. J. wrinkled his nose.

"He may find it a little harder to get into this race with an overweight car," said Father.

"Do you think his car will be disqualified?" asked T. J.

"I wouldn't be surprised," Father nodded.

"Wow! With Anthony gone, I'd have a good chance of winning!" T. J. exclaimed. "This is so exciting! I never thought I'd get another chance!"

T. J. did not feel quite so confident when he woke up the morning of the race. As he lay in bed with his arms wrapped around Sergeant's neck, T. J. began to worry. Why did he think it would be so easy to win against all of the best cars in the county? How could he possibly hope to come in first?

When Zack and Aaron arrived at his house, T. J. felt a little better. His friends were going with him, and they were good support.

"All aboard!" Father called to the boys when it was time to leave for the mall. Mother was going to come a little later with Charley and the girls.

When they got to the mall, T. J. and his friends whistled at the gigantic Pinewood Derby exhibition. It covered one whole floor of the Kingswood Shopping Mall.

"Hey, look!" T. J. exclaimed. "There's a television camera over there!"

The boys stared as a crew of newspeople set up

cameras and lights. T. J.'s stomach began to churn. Was he really going to race his car on television?

Just then someone picked up a microphone and began calling out pack numbers to report to the weigh-in station. When Pack Sixteen was called, T. J. got in line at one of the designated tables. A little ways ahead of him stood Anthony and his father. T. J. pointed him out to his father and friends.

"Let's watch and see if they let Anthony's car into the race," Father whispered to the boys.

They stood quietly and watched as Anthony made his way to the front of the line. When it was his turn, he handed his flashy orange car to the man seated behind the scales.

"I'm sorry, son," they heard the man say to Anthony, "but your car is too heavy."

"What do you mean too heavy?" Anthony's father barked.

"The car weighs five and one-eighth ounces," the man replied. "The weight limit is five ounces."

"What does an eighth of an ounce matter?" Anthony's father spluttered.

"An eighth of an ounce can make quite a difference in these little cars," the man tried to explain.

"Let's try a different set of scales," huffed Anthony's father.

"Okay," the other man sighed. He reached over and placed the car on another set of scales. "Five and one-eighth ounces," he announced.

"Humph!" Anthony's father snorted. He grabbed the car and marched away.

T. J., Zack, and Aaron had big smiles on their faces.

"I'm afraid Anthony and his father had that one coming," remarked Father.

When T. J. had his car weighed, it measured exactly five ounces. Breathing a sigh of relief, T. J. moved to the area set up for the first race.

T. J.'s first race was not his last. He moved to so many different tracks that he actually lost count of how many races in which his car had raced. All he knew was that he kept on winning!

Finally there was a pause in the races. Everyone was getting ready for the last two races. There would be eight contenders in the first race. The top three winners would then race for the first, second, and third place trophies.

Cameras rolled as the television announcer described the upcoming races to his viewers. T. J. stood on a raised platform with the seven other boys. He beamed at his parents. His mother clapped and cheered for him. His father gave him another thumbs-up victory sign.

The judge called for silence and the cars were loaded behind the gates of the race track. Everyone tensed as the countdown began, "five, four, three, two, one!"

"Oh, please, Lord Jesus, let me win!" T. J. prayed hurriedly.

The gates were opened and the cars shot down the tracks. The crowd went wild. Everyone shouted for their favorite car to win. T. J. did not hear any of it. He could only stare as his blue, red, and yellow car nosed its way across the finish line first, barely beating out a green car.

He won! He had won the first race! T. J. could hardly believe it. Could he do it again? Could he possibly become the winner of the county-wide Pinewood Derby?

While waiting for the last and final race, T. J. could look at no one but his father. His father had shared all of the pain and the joy of building this race car. Only he could understand how T. J. felt at this moment.

T. J. smiled as he remembered when his father had taken him to the Lathams' to get the block of wood shaped. He remembered how he and his father had scraped away the Sesame Street® stickers that T. J.'s little sisters had plastered all over his car. Father had also bought another whole kit after T. J. had messed up the first set of wheels, and he had helped T. J. get the wheels on right. Never before had T. J. felt so thankful for his father.

"And now, ladies and gentlemen," boomed the scoutmaster in charge of the race, "are you ready for the final race?"

The crowd answered with a mighty roar. T. J. grinned at his father as his car was loaded into gate number one.

"Five, four, three, two, one!" roared the scout-master.

Keeping his eyes glued to the race track, T. J. held his breath and prayed for his car to win. Would it be able to nose out the green car again?

Yes! The blue streak crossed the finish line well ahead of the green streak. He had won! T. J. had won!

A great shriek of joy sounded as T. J.'s family and friends rushed up onto the platform and grabbed him in one giant victorious hug.

"I'm so proud of you, son!" his father cried as he scooped up T. J. in his arms.

"I couldn't have done it without you, Dad," T. J. said as he grabbed his father around the neck and hugged him tightly.

Father laughed. "Now do you see what happens when you let God handle your problems?"

"You bet!" T. J. replied. "He really is awesome!"

Amen.

Adam Straight to the Rescue

Ketchup on pancakes?

Adam has always wanted brothers and sisters . . . but this ready-made family isn't quite what he had in mind. Three-year-old Jory is cute enough, although his fascination with meat-eating dinosaurs can get out of hand. But ten-year-old Belinda is another story. How can Adam put up with a sister who calls his mother E. S. (short for Evil Stepmother), makes up stories just to scare him, and eats ketchup on everything?

"When we get back from our camping trip," his mom assures him, "it'll seem like we've been together forever." Adam's not so sure, although the two-day trip packs enough adventure to last most families a lifetime. And in spite of—or maybe because of—runaway cars, midnight animal visitors, and trips to the emergency room, Adam does some serious thinking and praying about what it means to be a brother. As he says, "I don't know why I argue with You, God. It's hard work. And besides, You always win!"

K.R. Hamilton lives with her husband and kids in Birmingham, Alabama. She has worked as a ranch hand, a lumberjack, a census taker, and an archeological surveyor, among other things. She's not likely to run out of things to write about.

Adam Straight and the Mysterious Neighbor

Listen to the "Spider Lady"?

Adam isn't sure he wants to do yardwork for Miss Winters. She lives in a run-down old house on an overgrown lot, doesn't want him knocking on the door, and warns him to stay out of the fenced-in backyard. And now a strange man in a black suit calls her the Spider Lady! Something creepy is going on here.

But Adam needs the money, thanks to his stepsister Belinda's latest successful attempt to get him into trouble. And working with his new friend, Pelican, will be fun. But before Adam even realizes how it happened, he's become something of a spider himself—spinning a web of half-truths and misunderstandings that make Belinda even angrier and may cost him Pelican's friendship.

Before the mystery is solved, Adam finds that he and Belinda aren't so different after all . . . and that God's forgiveness is something a Christian needs—and can count on—time and time again.

K. R. Hamilton lives with her husband and kids in Birmingham, Alabama. She has worked as a ranch hand, a lumberjack, a census taker, and an archeological surveyor, among other things. She's not likely to run out of things to write about.

Project Cockroach

"We'll go down in Jefferson School history."

That's what Ben Anderson promises when he gets Josh to agree to his plan. And turning loose a horde of cockroaches in Mrs. Bannister's desk drawer does sound impressive. Josh knows what Wendell, his peculiar next-door neighbor and classmate, would say, but what would you expect from a kid who actually goes to the library in the summertime?

Josh's mom wants him to be a good student and stay out of trouble. His long-distance dad back in Woodview wants him to "have a good year." Wendell wants him to go to church. But Josh isn't sure that even God can help him find answers to the questions in his life. He just wants to make a few friends and fit into his new world . . . even if it means taking a risk or two.

ELAINE K. McEWAN, an elementary school principal and the mother of two grown children, knows a lot of kids like Josh.

Chariot Books
David C. Cook Publishing Co.

The Best Defense

"You sure know how to make a mother worry."

Josh has lived in Grandville barely two months, and he's already met the paramedics, the police, some teenaged would-be thugs, and a long-haired leather worker named Sonny. No wonder his mom gets a little anxious from time to time.

Josh thinks karate lessons would take care of some of his worries, but they aren't likely to help his relationship with Samantha Sullivan, the bossiest kid in the fifth grade. And they won't make his dad call more often.

Sonny tells him the key to conquering his fear is prayer . . . but Josh isn't sure that prayer is the answer. He needs to explore the possiblility. What if it doesn't work in a dark tunnel when he's facing two thugs?

ELAINE K. McEWAN, an elementary school principal and the mother of two grown children, knows a lot of kids like Josh.

Chariot Books®
David C. Cook Publishing Co.